Beavers

by Elizabeth O'Sullivan

Lerner Publications Company • Minneapolis

For Ian, Emily, and David

The images in this book are used with the permission of: © Thomas & Pat Leeson/Photo Researchers, Inc., pp. 4, 29; © Laura Westlund/Independent Picture Service, p. 5; © age fotostock/SuperStock, pp. 6, 19; © Leonard Lee Rue III/Photo Researchers, Inc., p. 7; © Steve Maslowski/Visuals Unlimited, p. 8; © Prisma/SuperStock, p. 9; © Karlene Schwartz, pp. 10, 11, 15, 17, 18, 20, 23, 24, 26, 36, 38, 40, 41, 42, 43, 48 (bottom); © Paul Glendell/Peter Arnold, Inc., p. 12; © Alan & Sandy Carey/Peter Arnold, Inc., p. 13; © Science VU/Visuals Unlimited, p. 14; © Ned Therrien/Visuals Unlimited, pp. 16, 48 (top); © Robert & Jean Pollock/Visuals Unlimited, p. 21; © Harry Engel/Photo Researchers, Inc., p. 22; © Lynda Richardson/Peter Arnold, Inc., pp. 25, 28, 30, 31, 32, 33, 35; © Carlyn Galati/Visuals Unlimited, p. 27; © Ed Cesar/Photo Researchers, Inc., p. 34; © Joe McDonald/Visuals Unlimited, p. 37; © Ron Spomer/Visuals Unlimited, p. 39; © Bill Banaszewski/Visuals Unlimited, pp. 46, 47.

Front Cover: © Tom McHugh/Photo Researchers, Inc.

Lerner Publications Company
A division of Lerner Publishing Group
241 First Avenue North
Minneapolis, MN 55401 U.S.A.

Website address: www.lernerbooks.com

Library of Congress Cataloging-in-Publication Data

O'Sullivan, Elizabeth, 1973–
    Beavers / by Elizabeth O'Sullivan.
        p.   cm. — (Early bird nature books)
    Includes index.
    ISBN-13: 978–0–8225–6465–2 (lib. bdg. : alk. paper)
    ISBN-10: 0–8225–6465–3 (lib. bdg. : alk. paper)
    1. Beavers—Juvenile literature. I. Title. II. Series.
QL737.R632O87 2007
599.37—dc22   2006006454

Manufactured in the United States of America
1 2 3 4 5 6 – JR – 12 11 10 09 08 07

Contents

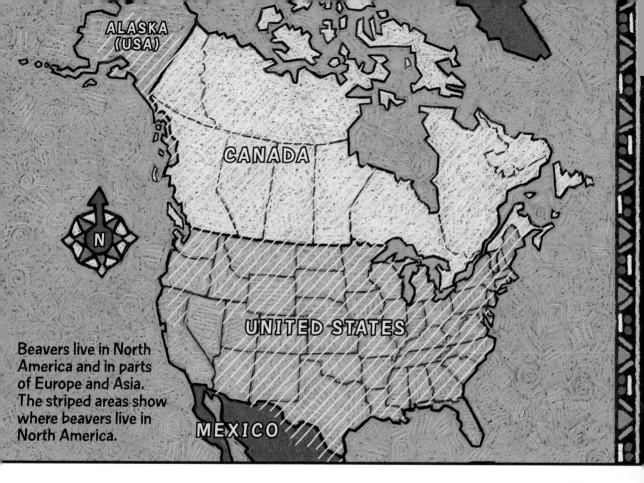

Beavers live in North America and in parts of Europe and Asia. The striped areas show where beavers live in North America.

Be a Word Detective

Can you find these words as you read about the beaver's life? Be a detective and try to figure out what they mean. You can turn to the glossary on page 46 for help.

aquatic	incisors	nocturnal
castoreum	kits	predators
colonies	lodge	rodents
dams	mammals	scent mound
dens	membranes	webbed

Chapter 1

All beavers are mammals. What is a mammal?

Beavers

Beavers are busy animals. They cut down trees near ponds and streams. Then they build things with the branches. They build dams across rivers. And they build big homes that stick out of the water.

Beavers are mammals. Mammals are animals that have hair and that feed their babies milk. Beavers belong to a group of mammals called rodents (ROH-duhnts). Squirrels, mice, and rats are rodents too.

All rodents have big front teeth called incisors (ihn-SEYE-zuhrz). These teeth are always growing longer. Chewing on things such as wood wears the teeth down. So the teeth never become too long.

A beaver's front teeth have hard, orange coverings. The coverings make the teeth strong.

Most rodents are smaller than beavers.
Beavers often weigh between 30 and 90 pounds.
Beavers can grow up to 4 feet long. That's
about as tall as a first grader.

Beavers are the largest rodents in North America.

Beavers are very good swimmers. This beaver is carrying a branch while it swims.

Beavers are aquatic (uh-KWAH-tihk). Aquatic animals spend much of their time in the water. When they swim underwater, beavers hold their breath. Beavers can hold their breath longer than people can. Beavers can hold their breath for 15 minutes!

A beaver uses its tail to steer while swimming. A beaver also uses its tail to balance when it is on land.

A beaver's back feet are webbed like a duck's feet. Webbed feet help the beaver to swim. A wide, flat tail helps the beaver steer while swimming. The tail looks a little like a paddle. Clear membranes (MEM-braynz) cover a beaver's eyes while it is underwater. Membranes are like very thin skin. A beaver's membranes work like goggles. They protect the eyes from water.

Brown, thick fur keeps beavers warm. The fur keeps beavers dry too. Water cannot get through a beaver's fur. Oil on the fur keeps the water out. A beaver's body makes the oil. It comes out near the beaver's tail. The oil is called castoreum (kas-TAWR-ee-uhm). Beavers rub castoreum all over their fur.

A beaver's fur has two layers. It is very thick.

Beavers always live near water. Some beavers live in North America. Canada and the United States are home to many beavers. Other beavers live in parts of Europe and Asia.

Beavers that live in the United States and Canada are called American Beavers. Beavers that live in Europe and Asia are called Eurasian beavers. This beaver lives in Europe.

Chapter 2

Beavers bite into trees. They make the trees fall down. How do beavers cut down trees?

Home and Food

Can you imagine cutting down a tree with your teeth? Beavers do that. A beaver cuts down a tree by biting into the tree's trunk. The beaver makes cuts in the trunk. It rips out pieces of wood until the tree falls down. Cutting down a big tree takes weeks of work. But cutting a tiny tree takes just a few minutes.

Beavers cut down trees to get the branches. Beavers drag the branches back to their homes. Dragging big branches is hard work. To make it easier, beavers might dig canals. Canals are paths dug for water to flow through. Beavers use canals to float branches back to their homes.

Beavers work hard cutting and carrying branches. Because of this, people say that a busy person is "busy as a beaver."

The pile of branches on the right is a beaver lodge.

Beavers use big branches to build their homes. They use rocks and mud too. A beaver's home is called a lodge. Beavers often build lodges in ponds or lakes. A lodge's top is 3 to 6 feet above the water. The bottom of the lodge is underwater. The lodge is often more than 10 feet wide at the bottom. That is wider than some bedrooms.

To get inside their lodge, beavers swim through underwater tunnels. Then they pop up through holes in the lodge's floor. Beaver lodges are dry inside. They stay warm, even during cold winters. Lodges often have two rooms. Sometimes beavers eat in one room and sleep in another.

It looks like there is no way to go inside a beaver lodge.
But underwater tunnels let beavers in.

Beavers work together to build things.

Beavers live together in groups called colonies (KOL-uh-neez). A colony works together to build a lodge. First, the colony makes a pile of sticks. The pile starts deep underwater. It ends high above the water. Then the colony chews tunnels and rooms inside the pile. The rooms stay dry because they are above the water. The beavers cover the floor with mud and plants. They cover the outside of the lodge with mud too.

The two walls made of branches are beaver dams. A beaver colony in New Hampshire built these dams.

Sometimes beavers can't find a pond for their lodge. Then they make one themselves. They find a stream or river. They use branches, mud, and rocks to build a wall across the water. This dam keeps water from flowing. A pond forms behind the dam. Beavers can build their lodge in this pond.

Some rivers flow too fast to be stopped by a beaver dam. Beavers cannot build their lodges on those rivers. Instead, the beavers dig deep holes in the riverbank. Then they live in the holes. These beaver homes are called dens.

Some beavers make their homes on riverbanks. This beaver is eating on a riverbank.

Beavers sometimes eat water lilies. Water lilies grow in beaver ponds.

Beavers are nocturnal (nok-TUR-nuhl). Nocturnal animals sleep during the day. And they are awake at night. Beavers look for food at night.

Beavers eat only plants. During the summer, they eat fresh plants. Moss, leaves, and buds are their favorite summer foods.

In the winter, beavers eat tree bark. They gather branches during the fall. Then they drag them underwater. The beavers stick the branches into the bottom of the pond. The branches can't float away. Cold water keeps branches fresh for many months.

Beavers stuck these branches into the bed of a stream. They stored them to eat in the cold winter months.

The top of a pond freezes during the winter. Beavers swim in the cold water under the ice. When they are hungry, they carry some branches back to the lodge. They eat them inside. The beavers hold the branches with their front paws. They nibble off the bark. It looks as if they are eating corn on the cob.

Beavers use their paws to hold their food.

Chapter 3

Beavers tell other beavers when danger is near. How do beavers warn one another about dangers?

Beaver Talk

Do you know what would happen if you surprised a beaver? The beaver would surprise you back! When a beaver is afraid, it slaps its flat tail on the water. This makes a very loud bang. Other beavers hear the slap. They understand that danger is near. And they hurry into the water. The beavers are safer there.

A beaver might use its voice to talk to other beavers.

Beavers also tell one another things with
their voices. Beaver talk sounds like barks,
growls, whines, and moans. Baby beavers are
louder than the adults.

Beavers have other ways of talking too. They often use touch. Sometimes beavers touch their faces together. People call this kissing.

Beavers are social animals.

This small pile is a beaver's scent (SENT) mound.

Beavers use smell to talk to beavers that are not part of their colony. They do this by making a scent mound. First, a beaver makes a small pile of dirt. Then it squirts castoreum on the pile. The castoreum has a strong smell. Other beavers smell the scent on the dirt mound. Then they know that a colony of beavers lives nearby.

Beavers help to take care of one another's fur. This is called grooming. Beavers use their mouths to groom one another. They clean one another's fur and spread oil on it. Beavers spend a lot of time grooming every day.

These beavers are grooming each other's fur.

Chapter 4

The small animals on the right are baby beavers. What are baby beavers called?

Raising Babies

Mother beavers have babies every year. The babies are called kits. Newborn kits weigh about 1 pound. That is as heavy as a man's tennis shoe. Mother beavers usually have two to six kits.

The kits drink milk from their mother for several weeks. But after a few days, baby beavers begin to eat plants and bark too. Adults gather food to share with the babies.

These kits are drinking their mother's milk. The mother eats as she feeds her babies.

Kits stay inside the lodge for several weeks. Their mother, father, and older brothers and sisters take care of them. Beaver families never leave the babies alone.

A young beaver guards its smaller brothers and sisters.

Sometimes kits get into trouble. They jump into water in the lodge's tunnels. But an adult drags them out of the water. Baby beavers float. But the water might make them too cold.

Adult beavers carry kits in their mouths.

Beavers talk to one another inside their lodges.

Baby beavers are loud. They whine for food. The adults talk to the kits too. They growl softly. Adults seem to scold the kits sometimes. It sounds as if the adults are barking.

These young beavers are swimming with their mother.

When the kits are one or two months old, they are big enough to go outside. They can swim without getting cold. Their family stays very close to them. The older beavers protect the babies from other animals.

Young beavers learn by helping.

When young beavers are about one year
old, they begin helping their colony. They help
cut down trees and gather branches. They also
help fix the dam and the lodge. And they take
care of their younger brothers and sisters.

Most young beavers live with their parents for two years. Then they leave the colony. They are ready to start families of their own.

This beaver has reached adulthood.

Chapter 5

Wolves hunt and eat beavers. What is the name for animals that hunt and eat other animals?

Trouble for Beavers

 Wolves, bears, and coyotes hunt and eat beavers. Animals that hunt and eat other animals are called predators (PREH-duh-turz).

Beavers cannot run fast. So it is easy for predators to catch beavers when they are on land. But beavers swim fast. So beavers are safer from predators in the water. They are safest of all in their lodge.

Beavers go into ponds and streams to get away from predators.

This fur is from a beaver. Hats made of beaver fur were once very popular.

People cause more trouble for beavers than predators do. In the past, many people trapped beavers for their fur. Beavers' soft, thick fur was very expensive. People trapped as many beavers as they could. Finally, beavers were gone from most of the United States. They disappeared from many countries in Europe too.

People made laws to protect beavers. Then they brought beavers back to where they used to live. The beavers had families there. More and more kits were born. Finally, beavers lived in most of the same places as before.

Beavers have returned to their original homes.

Beavers cause problems for people too. Sometimes beavers cut down trees that people want. And beavers make ponds where people don't want them. These ponds may cover farm fields and roads.

Beavers can cause a lot of damage to trees.

This family of ducks lives in a beaver pond.

But in other places, beaver ponds are helpful. They make good places for many animals and plants to live. Ducks have their families in beaver ponds. Fish live there. And water lilies and other plants grow there.

Beaver dams can also be helpful. Beaver dams slow down fast streams. Fast streams sometimes wash away too much soil. If too much soil washes away, plants cannot grow.

Beaver dams such as this one slow down the flow of streams.

Beavers are very busy creatures.

Beavers take good care of their families. And they work hard to have safe homes. Their work changes the way the world looks. They make new ponds that help other animals. Busy as a beaver is a nice thing to be.

ON SHARING A BOOK

When you share a book with a child, you show that reading is important. To get the most out of the experience, read in a comfortable, quiet place. Turn off the television and limit other distractions, such as telephone calls.

Be prepared to start slowly. Take turns reading parts of this book. Stop occasionally and discuss what you're reading. Talk about the photographs. If the child begins to lose interest, stop reading. When you pick up the book again, revisit the parts you have already read.

BE A VOCABULARY DETECTIVE

The word list on page 5 contains words that are important in understanding of the topic of this book. Be word detectives and search for the words as you read the book together. Talk about what the words mean and how they are used in the sentence. Do any of these words have more than one meaning? You will find the words defined in a glossary on page 46.

WHAT ABOUT QUESTIONS?

Use questions to make sure the child understands the information in this book. Here are some suggestions:

> What did this paragraph tell us? What does this picture show? What do you think we'll learn about next? Where do beavers live? Could a beaver live in your backyard? Why/why not? How do beavers build their homes? What do beavers eat? What are baby beavers called? What is your favorite part of this book? Why?

If the child has questions, don't hesitate to respond with questions of your own such as What do *you* think? Why? What is it that you don't know? If the child can't remember certain facts, turn to the index.

INTRODUCING THE INDEX

The index helps readers find information without searching through the whole book. Turn to the index on page 48. Choose an entry such as *size* and ask the child to use the index to find out how big beavers are. Repeat this exercise with as many entries as you like. Ask the child to point out the differences between an index and a glossary. (The index helps readers find information, while the glossary tells readers what words mean.)

LEARN MORE ABOUT
BEAVERS

BOOKS

Hodge, Deborah. *Beavers*. Tonawanda, NY: Kids Can Press, 1998. This book includes detailed drawings and lots of fun facts about beavers.

Marie, Christian. *Little Beavers*. Milwaukee: Gareth Stevens Publishing, 2006. In this book, you can follow the baby beaver from birth until it is old enough to leave home.

Rounds, Glen. *Beaver*. New York: Holiday House, 1999. This illustrated book discusses the beaver's behavior.

Taylor, Bonnie Highsmith. *Gus: A Beaver*. Logan, IA: Perfection Learning, 2001. Read about the life of a beaver in this interesting book.

WEBSITES

Critter Guide: Beaver
http://www.pbs.org/wnet/nature/critters/beaver.html
This public television site includes facts about where beavers live, what they eat, and how they behave.

Enchanted Learning: North American Beaver
http://www.enchantedlearning.com/subjects/mammals/Beaver.shtml
Visit this site to learn about beavers' homes, food, predators, and more.

GLOSSARY

aquatic (uh-KWAH-tihk): living in the water

castoreum (kas-TAWR-ee-uhm): a smelly oil that comes from a beaver's body

colonies (KOL-uh-neez): beaver families

dams: walls of branches, mud, and rocks that beavers build to keep water from flowing. Beavers build dams to make safe places for their homes.

dens: deep holes in riverbanks where some beavers live

incisors (ihn-SEYE-zuhrz): big front teeth

kits: baby beavers

lodge: one type of beaver home. Beavers make lodges from branches, rocks, and mud.

mammals: animals that have hair and that feed their babies milk

membranes (MEM-braynz): thin, clear coverings on a beaver's eyes. Membranes protect a beaver's eyes when it is underwater.

nocturnal (nok-TUR-nuhl): animals that are active at night

predators (PREH-duh-turz): animals that hunt and eat other animals

rodents (ROH-duhnts): a group of small animals with big front teeth. Squirrels, mice, and beavers are rodents.

scent (SENT) mound: a pile of dirt on which a beaver leaves its smell. A beaver makes a scent mound to send a message to other beavers.

webbed: connected by a fold of skin. A beaver's back feet are webbed.

INDEX

Pages listed in **bold** type refer to photographs.